Cymbeline, King of Britain

Sweet Cherry

Publishing

Published by Sweet Cherry Publishing Limited
Unit E, Vulcan Business Complex,
Vulcan Road,
Leicester, LE5 3EB,
United Kingdom

First published in the USA in 2013
ISBN: 978-1-78226-070-7

©Macaw Books

Title: Cymbeline, King of Britain
North American Edition

Text & Illustration by Macaw Books 2013

www.sweetcherrypublishing.com

Printed and bound by Wai Man Book Binding (China) Ltd. Kowloon, H.K.

About Shakespeare

William Shakespeare, regarded as the greatest writer in the English language, was born in Stratford-upon-Avon in Warwickshire, England (around April 23, 1564). He was the third of eight children born to John and Mary Shakespeare.

Shakespeare was a poet, playwright, and dramatist. He is often known as England's national poet and the "Bard of Avon." Thirty-eight plays, 154 sonnets, two long narrative poems, and several other poems are attributed to him. Shakespeare's plays have been translated into every major existent language and are performed more often than those of any other playwright.

Cymbeline: He is the King of Britain and Imogen's father. He is a wise, gracious king. However, after the arrival of his new queen, he is led astray by her lies and wicked schemes.

Imogen: She is the daughter of King Cymbeline. She is beautiful, wise, and quick-witted. Imogen marries lowborn Posthumus against her father's wishes instead of Cloten, her father's stepson.

Iachimo: He is a clever, dishonest gentleman. He persuades Posthumus to enter into a wager with him, saying

that he will be able to seduce his wife, Imogen. He resorts to trickery in order to succeed.

Posthumus: He was orphaned as a child and has been raised by King Cymbeline. He falls in love with Imogen, the king's daughter, and marries her in secret. He is banished by the king and later believes Iachimo's lie that his wife has been unfaithful.

Cymbeline, King of Britain

At about the same time as Augustus Caesar ruled over the Roman Empire, there lived in England a king called Cymbeline.

Cymbeline's first wife had died when his three children

were very young. He had
two sons and a daughter.
However, tragedy had struck
in Cymbeline's life. His
daughter, Imogen, the eldest
of the three, grew up in her
father's court, but his two sons
were kept in the nursery and
had been kidnapped when
they were very young—the
elder one was around three
years old and the younger a

mere infant. It could never be ascertained what became of these two young boys.

Cymbeline had since married again. His second wife was a scheming witch, who treated Imogen cruelly. Though she hated Imogen, she often desired that Cymbeline's daughter be given in marriage to her son, Cloten, from a

previous marriage. Her plan
was simple. In the event
of Cymbeline's death, her
son could be anointed the
new King of England.

But Imogen realized what she was planning and therefore married quietly, without asking for the consent of her father or stepmother. Imogen's husband  was Posthumus, one of the best scholars and most accomplished men of the times. His was a sad story, for his father had died before he was even born, in a war fighting for Cymbeline. His mother too had passed away shortly after his birth, unable to bear the grief of her husband's death. He had been taken in by the great king himself and provided for ever since. Since his parents had died without giving him a name, Cymbeline named him Posthumus.

Imogen and Posthumus were taught by the same

teachers and had been very close since childhood. With the passing of time, their affection for each other blossomed into love, until such time as they decided to get married.

When the news reached the queen, who had employed several spies to keep tabs on

her stepdaughter, she was extremely angry, for her evil designs on Cymbeline's throne had been thwarted. She at once went to inform the king about the marriage of his daughter. Needless to say, Cymbeline was furious upon learning this news, based on the fact that

his daughter had forgotten
the dignity of her birth and
married a common subject
at his court. He banished
Posthumus at once, and the
poor scholar was forced to leave
his native country forever.

The queen then started
working on another plan to

meet her desires. She pretended to befriend Imogen and consoled her about the separation from her husband. She even went as far as to arrange a secret meeting between Posthumus and Imogen before the nobleman left for Rome.

She had decided that once
Posthumus was gone, she would
ask Imogen to marry her own
son, Cloten, as her earlier
marriage had been unlawful.

As the heartbroken pair
bade farewell, Imogen gave her
husband a diamond ring that
had belonged to her mother as a

token to remember her by, and he in turn placed a bracelet on her wrist, which she promised she would never take off.

Once Posthumus arrived in Rome, he met a group of young men who had come

from different parts of the
world. They talked about
their own loves and how the
ladies from their respective
countries were the most sought-
after women in the world.
Posthumus, remembering
his fair wife, recounted that
there could never be another
woman like Imogen.

However, one man among
those who had gathered there,
called Iachimo, did not like
what Posthumus said about
Imogen, as he was sure that
the ladies of Rome—his native
country— were far superior
to the women of Britain.
Posthumus soon made a wager,
whereby Iachimo would go to

Britain and try to woo Imogen. His task would be to obtain the bracelet that Posthumus had given Imogen, and Posthumus would then give him the ring Imogen had given him before leaving. However, if Iachimo did not succeed, he would have to give Posthumus a huge sum of money.

Iachimo was given a warm welcome by Imogen when she heard that he was a friend of her husband's. But when he tried to claim his love for her, Imogen started to ward him off. Iachimo realized that it would be nearly impossible to convince Imogen to give him

the bracelet as
a token of her
love. He also
knew that he
would stand to
lose a great deal if
he went back to Rome without
the bracelet. So he managed to

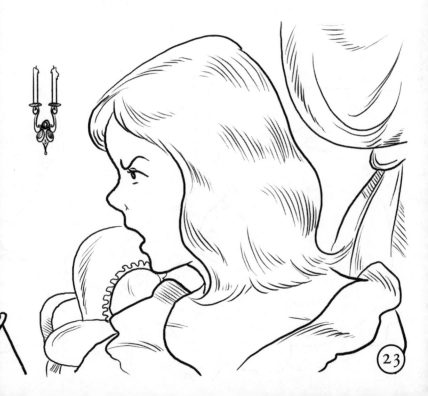

bribe Imogen's servants and hid himself in a trunk in her room.

That night, when Imogen finally fell asleep, Iachimo came out of hiding and started to make careful observations of the room. He even noted that Imogen had a small mole on her neck. Finally, he

gently removed the bracelet from her wrist and was gone.

When he returned to Rome, Iachimo made a song and dance about the way in which Imogen had responded to his charms, and how he had even met her in her own room after everyone had retired for the night. He went on to give a rather lengthy description

of her room, all of which Posthumus knew to be true.

Finally, Iachimo revealed the bracelet that was the principal clause of the wager and showed it to Posthumus, also describing the mole Imogen had on her neck. Posthumus was completely heartbroken to hear all this and, with a heavy heart, he gave away the diamond ring that Imogen had given him when she bade him farewell. Iachimo had successfully proved to Posthumus that Imogen's love for him was truly false.

Unable to calm his jealous rage against Imogen, Posthumus wrote to his friend Pisanio in Britain, who was an old friend of theirs. He recounted the tale of Imogen's betrayal and asked him to take her to Milford-Haven—a

seaport in Wales— and kill
her. He wrote another letter
to Imogen, declaring that his
love for her was so great that
he was returning to see her
again at Milford-Haven, braving
her father's orders against
him. Imogen, on receiving
the letter, unsuspectingly left
for the seaport with Pisanio.

But Pisanio, though
loyal to Posthumus, could
not bring himself to carry
out this shameful deed and
told Imogen of her husband's
orders. Imogen was completely
crestfallen. Pisanio comforted
her and told her of his plan to
make Posthumus pay for his
actions. He convinced her to

dress up like a
man and then
travel to Rome
to confront
her husband.

Pisanio had to
return to court before
he was missed. But before
leaving, he gave Imogen a vial

containing a special liquid
given to him by the queen.
Little did he know that the
queen, hating his closeness to
both Imogen and Posthumus,
had given him a vial of poison,
telling him that it was a special
medicine that could cure any
affliction. But the physician

from whom she had acquired it, knowing of the queen's evil ways, had made some changes to the composition. The liquid would put the person into a deep sleep, making everyone think that he or she was dead. Only later, when the potency

wore off, would the person
wake from their deep slumber.

Imogen soon set off for
Rome with this special tonic.
But destiny had other plans for
her. She lost her way and ended
up at the home of her brothers,
who had been kidnapped.

They had been taken by a man
called Bellarius, a lord at the
court of Cymbeline. He had
been falsely accused of treason
and, as revenge, had stolen the
infant princes. But hidden away
in his cave, he had grown fond

of them and raised them as his own children. It was now time for them to join the army.

Imogen, lost in the forest, had stumbled upon their cave, hungry and cold. Unable to continue any farther, she

stopped there to rest. Bellarius
and her two brothers found
her and took her in. They
offered her food, but when
she tried to give them money
for it, the noblemen refused.
They asked her where she was
going and what her name was.
Remember, all this time they
thought Imogen was a man.

Imogen replied that her name was Fidele and that she was bound for Italy, but the bad weather had made her lose her way. Bellarius immediately invited Fidele to come inside and share the venison they had brought back from their hunt. Fidele, it turned out, was an

excellent cook and was soon
able to charm his way into
the hearts of the three men.

After a while, Imogen,
who had grown
to love the two
boys like her
own brothers,
not knowing

their true identity, told them
that she was well rested and it
was time for her to continue her
journey to Italy from Milford-
Haven. Though she would
have loved to stay on with
them, she still had to confront
Posthumus over his evil actions.

But alas, she started to feel
a little unwell. The boys told

her to rest while they went into the forest and brought back some more food. No sooner did Bellarius and the boys leave than Imogen took a sip of the curing liquid that Pisanio had given her. Within a few minutes, she was sleeping in a deathlike slumber.

When the men returned,
Imogen's brother Polydore
was the first to enter the cave
and find Fidele dead. He was
very sad and behaved as if he
had known Fidele for a long
time. Bellarius, who had also
grown fond of the young boy,
decided to carry their guest to
the forest and bury him there.

But as the men left her in the forest and returned to their cave, the drug wore off and Imogen woke up. She wondered how she had come to be covered in flowers in the middle of the forest. She realized that perhaps she had dreamed the whole thing and set off immediately toward Milford-Haven. She

had decided she would seek out her husband like as a page and take up the matter with him.

But little did Imogen know of the developments that had taken place while she was away from the palace. Augustus Caesar, the supreme leader of Rome, had declared

war on Cymbeline of Britain and a large Roman Army had already landed in Britain. Posthumus was part of that army.

But Posthumus was not the same man who had ordered his wife to be killed. He had come back with the Roman Army not to fight for them, but against them. He still believed that his wife had been cruel to him, but news of her death following a letter from Pisanio weighed heavily

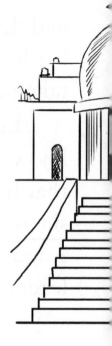

on his mind. He decided that he would fight the war, and either get killed fighting or be executed by Cymbeline for coming back to the country.

Before Imogen could reach the seaport, she was captured by the Roman Army and appointed as a page to Lucius, the valiant Roman general. Unknown to her, her brothers Polydore and Cadwal had joined the British Army along with their father, Bellarius, who had long repented for the injury he had caused Cymbeline by kidnapping his sons.

Finally, when the two armies fought, the British forces surely would have been defeated had it not been

for the bravery displayed by Posthumus, Bellarius, and the two brothers, who managed to save the king and let the battle be won in Britain's favor. Posthumus did not die fighting and handed himself over to one of Cymbeline's officers, agreeing to die for having disobeyed the king's

orders and having come back
to Britain against his wishes.

Imogen and her general
had been captured and
presented before Cymbeline, as
had Iachimo, the villain who
now served as a commander in
the Roman Army. Posthumus
too had been brought to
court to be punished for
returning. The noble Bellarius

and his two sons were also present, for they were to be rewarded for their gallantry.

Lucius, the Roman general, was the first to speak. He said that while he would gladly embrace death at the hands of his enemies, he begged that Imogen,

or Fidele as he called him,
be spared. He was after all
a British national and was
a good page. He begged
Cymbeline to spare him, even
if he spared no one else.

Cymbeline had not been
able to recognize his own
daughter because she was dressed

in male clothes, but he felt that there was some connection between him and this noble page. So  he forgave Imogen at once and agreed to give her anything she desired. Everyone turned to look at the page to see what she

would request from the king.
But all that she wanted to know
was how Iachimo had found the
ring that he now wore on his
finger, the same ring
that she had given
to Posthumus.

Cymbeline
was only too

glad to grant her this wish and
threatened Iachimo with torture
if he did not confess. Iachimo,
who was already scared in the
presence of the king, told them
everything, from accepting
the wager from Posthumus
to deceiving Imogen and
Posthumus. When Posthumus

heard this news he was completely shattered. He immediately confessed his crime before the king and wept profusely.

Imogen now understood her husband's actions and forgave him. She realized that he too had been deceived. She immediately revealed herself to the people and the court, and Cymbeline was beside himself with joy for having finally found his daughter again. He was so happy that not only

did he pardon Posthumus,
but he even acknowledged
their wedding and accepted
him as his son-in-law.

Bellarius chose this joyous
moment to confess about his
sons and presented the king's
own long-lost sons before him.
Obviously the king did not
consider punishing Bellarius,

because he had brought only
joy to him that day. Now that
everything had been resolved,
Imogen asked her father
to also forgive the Roman
general Lucius, and
with his help,
Britain and Rome
signed a successful
peace treaty.

Everyone was finally
happy with the way
things had turned out.

The evil queen, though,
died from depression,
since none of her plans
had succeeded!